Clarion Books
a Houghton Mifflin Company imprint
215 Park Avenue South, New York, NY 10003
Text and illustrations copyright © 2006 by Clavis Uitgeverij Amsterdam-Hasselt.
English language translation copyright © 2007 by Houghton Mifflin Company.

First published as *Sarah en Haar Spookjes* in Belgium in 2006
by Clavis Uitgeverij. First American edition, 2007.

The illustrations were executed in oils.
The text was set in 20-point Angie.

For information about permission to reproduce selections from this book,
write to Permissions, Houghton Mifflin Company, 215 Park Avenue South,
New York, NY 10003.

www.clarionbooks.com

Printed in Slovenia.

Library of Congress Cataloging-in-Publication Data

Robberecht, Thierry.
[Sarah en haar spookjes. English]
Sarah's little ghosts / by Thierry Robberecht ; illustrated by Philippe Goossens.—1st American ed.
p. cm.
Summary: When Sarah breaks her mother's favorite necklace and then does not tell the truth,
little ghosts that only she can see begin to interfere with her life.
ISBN-13: 978-0-618-89210-5
ISBN-10: 0-618-89210-9
[1. Honesty—Fiction.] I. Goossens, Philippe, ill. II. Title.
PZ7.R53233Sar 2007
[E]—dc22
2006031147

10 9 8 7 6 5 4 3 2 1

Sarah's Little Ghosts

by Thierry Robberecht

Illustrated by Philippe Goossens

Clarion Books
New York

I love playing with Mom's jewelry. I'm allowed to wear all of it—except her favorite necklace. It belonged to Grandma, and it has the most beautiful beads. It's my favorite, too, so sometimes I sneak into Mom's room and try it on anyway.

Today, though, the string breaks in my hands. *Whoosh!* The little beads go flying everywhere!

I quickly pick them all up and hide them in the back of the drawer. Maybe Mom won't notice. I'm sure not going to tell her.

But when I see Mom, I can't talk to her or look in her eyes.

"Is something wrong, Sarah?" she asks.

"No. Nothing," I say.

But along with the words something else comes out of my mouth. *Pop!*

It's a little ghost!

The ghost flies around the room singing, "I broke your necklace! I broke your necklace!"

"Shh!" I say. "What if Mom hears you?"

But it seems only I can hear the ghost. I wish I couldn't.

15

After dinner, Dad and I sit on the couch. Usually we cuddle together and tell funny stories or read a book. But tonight something sits between us. That little ghost is starting to bother me.

I can't fall asleep because of the ghost's noise. It flies around my room, singing, "I broke your necklace! I broke your necklace!"

"Who *are* you?" I ask. "Why don't you leave me alone?"

"I'm the ghost of secrets," it answers. "I say the words you want to say but are too scared to."

"You don't scare me," I tell it. But the words of its song *do* scare me.

19

When I wake up the next morning, that awful little ghost is sitting on my tummy! I run to the kitchen—and bump right into Mom.

"Do you know where my favorite necklace is, Sarah?" she asks. "I can't find it anywhere."

"No," I answer. "I don't know where it is."

Then, *Pop!* Another little ghost flies out of my mouth.

"I hid your necklace!" sings this one.

"Shh!" I say.

21

I can't wait to go to school. But the two little ghosts follow me out the door. They fly behind me, shouting their songs.

At school, my friends ask if something is wrong. "No. Nothing," I say. And out flies another little ghost. *Pop!*

Then the teacher asks why I'm crying. *Pop!* They're everywhere!

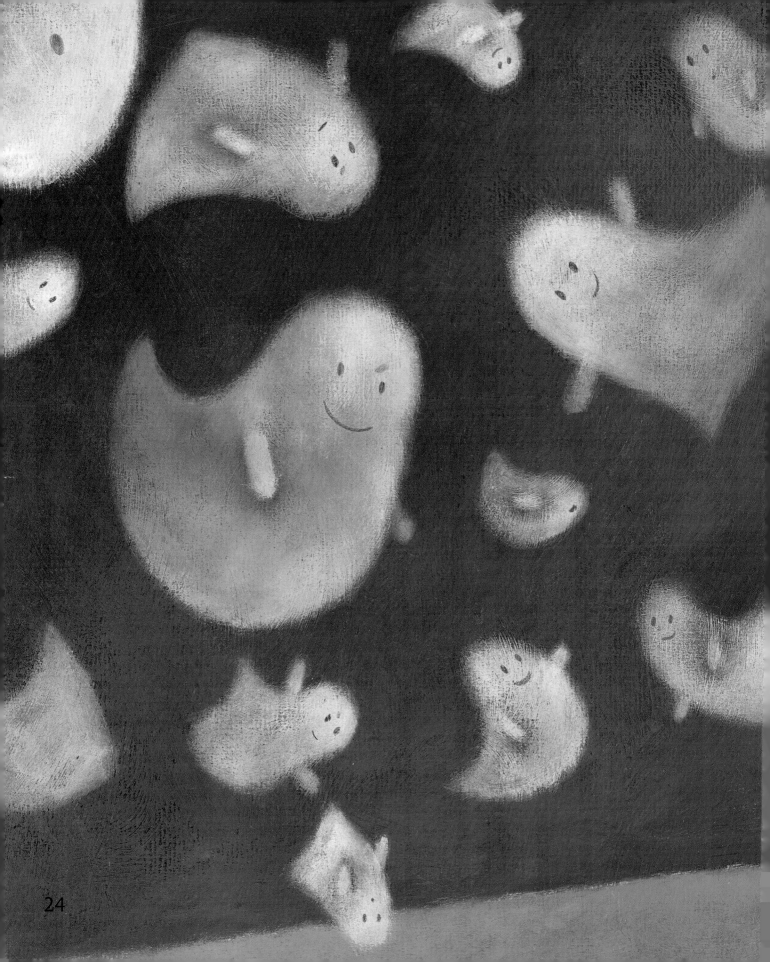

By the time I get home from school, I feel like I'm living in a haunted house. I try talking to Mom, but the ghosts' singing is too loud. I try cuddling with Dad, but the ghosts keep getting in the way. Finally, I go sit in the corner by myself.

25

Soon Mom comes over.

"I found my necklace," she says. "It was broken and hidden in the back of the drawer. Do you know what happened to it, Sarah?"

All the ghosts are circling around me, but the first ghost is singing the loudest.

"I broke your necklace," I say. "I'm sorry."

Poof! The first ghost is gone.

So I tell Mom the truth about everything else that happened, and the ghosts disappear, one by one. *Poof! Poof! Poof!*

Dad helps me put the necklace back together.
Mom smiles when we give it to her and gives me
a big hug in return. It feels good not to have those
secrets between us anymore. The ghosts still pop up
from time to time, but they don't stay long. Now I
know the magic words to make them disappear. I tell
the truth. Then *Poof!*